Robert finds a way

Author: Seuling, Barbara.
Reading Level: 4.0 LG
Point Value: 2.0
ACCELERATED READER QUIZ 110593

Robert
Finds
a Way

Also by Barbara Seuling

Oh No, It's Robert

Robert and the Great Pepperoni

Robert and the Weird & Wacky Facts

Robert and the Back-to-School Special

Robert and the Lemming Problem

Robert and the Great Escape

Robert Takes a Stand

Robert Finds a Way

by Barbara Seuling
Illustrated by Paul Brewer

Cricket Books

Chicago

Library of Congress Cataloging-in-Publication Data

Seuling, Barbara.
  Robert finds a way / by Barbara Seuling ; illustrated by Paul Brewer.— 1st ed.
     p. cm.
  Summary: Robert's parents and brother are always using the computer when he needs it to research school projects, but eventually the family finds a way to solve the problem.
  ISBN 0-8126-2734-2
  [1. Problem solving—Fiction. 2. Resourcefulness—Fiction. 3. Computers—Fiction. 4. Schools—Fiction. 5. Family life—New Jersey—Fiction. 6. New Jersey—Fiction.] I. Brewer, Paul, 1950-, ill. II. Title.
  PZ7.S5135Rs 2005
  [Fic]—dc22
                                         2004020104

for Tracy Gripentrog
and all the lucky kids who get to be in her class
—B. S.

for Ken and Ginny
—P. B.

Contents

A Bad Start   1

The Bad Fairy   11

Mouth Torture   17

Baby Food   23

Loose Wire   29

Emergency!   40

A Mess   45

Hamburger Again   51

Paul's Back   57

Wonder Dogs   67

Obstacle Course   76

E-mail Buddies   85

The Hoop   92

Ice Fishing   106

White Bear   118

From Bad to Worse   126

The Letter   133

Kirby   139

At Last!   143

A Bad Start

R-R-RRRRING!

Robert Dorfman awoke from a sound sleep and threw off the covers. Huckleberry, his dog, landed with a thump on the floor.

Robert stumbled over the blanket and the dog to the alarm clock on his dresser to shut it off. He kept the clock far away from his bed so he'd be sure to get up when it rang. Otherwise, he'd just shut it off, turn over, and go back to sleep.

He scratched his dog's head as they made their way to the bathroom. Huckleberry followed him everywhere. Oh no. The door was locked. Robert knocked. No answer. He knocked again. He pounded on the door.

"What?" came the voice from inside.

"Come on, Charlie. I have to brush my teeth now," Robert called. He was going to be late.

"CHARLIE!" he shouted.

Huckleberry barked.

At last the door opened. Charlie, still wearing his headphones, backed against the wall as Huckleberry moved toward him, still barking.

"Take away your attack dog!" said Charlie.

Robert had to laugh. Attack dog! Huckleberry was no attack dog. But Robert didn't mind having a dog who helped him out, as he had just then.

After he got dressed, Robert thumped down the stairs and into the kitchen. He let Huckleberry out the door into the backyard.

"Good morning, Rob," said his mom.

"Good morning," he answered, digging the scoop into the dog food bag to fill Huckleberry's bowl. Robert watched his brother slug down a glass of orange juice, then jump up to leave. When Robert got to the table, he reached for the container. He poured, but nothing came out.

"Is there any more orange juice?" he asked.

"I'm afraid not," said his mom. "I'll put it on the shopping list."

She got up and wrote something on a pad on the refrigerator door, with a pencil that hung from it. "Would you like some grapefruit juice?" she asked.

Robert slumped in his chair. "No, thanks." He hated grapefruit juice. He chewed the edges of a toaster tart around and around until it was just the soft middle. Then he ate that part last, washing it down with milk.

Robert's mom put a brown paper bag next to his plate. "Don't forget your lunch," she reminded him.

"Thanks," he answered, slipping off his chair and into his jacket. He stuffed the lunch bag into his backpack and kissed his mom good-bye.

"See you later," she said. "Have a good day."

"Thanks," said Robert again, slinging the backpack over his shoulder. He waved a good-bye behind him as he ran down the path. He felt grumpy, but he knew things would get better once he met up with Paul. Every morning Paul Felcher, his best friend, waited for Robert on Paul's corner, and they walked to school together. They only took the bus if the weather was bad.

Could it be? Paul wasn't there. But Paul was always there. Unless . . . That must be it. The last time Paul wasn't there was when he was out sick.

Robert dragged his feet, walking the long blocks to school alone. It felt as though his sneakers had cement in them.

In the classroom, Robert put his backpack in his space at Table Four, where he sat with Vanessa Nicolini next to him and Paul across from him. Except today. Paul's chair was empty.

Being in Mrs. Bernthal's classroom could usually cheer Robert up, but today he was worried. Mrs. Bernthal walked over to the monitors chart.

"Class, I'd like your attention, please," said Mrs. Bernthal, as the children settled down. "It's the first of the month and time to choose new monitors. Our present monitors have done an excellent job, so let's give them all a hand," she added. Everyone applauded.

Mrs. Bernthal pointed at the first category: PLANTS.

"Who would like to be the next plant monitor?" she asked.

Vanessa's hand went up.

"Excellent. Anyone else?" She looked around. Pamela Rose raised her hand.

"Good. Vanessa and Pamela," said Mrs. Bernthal. "You are our new plant monitors.

Thank you." She wrote the two names next to PLANTS.

Next, Mrs. Bernthal pointed to CLOTHING CLOSET. Lucy Ritts waved her hand. Brian Hoberman stuck his hand up, too. "Thank you Lucy and Brian." Mrs. Bernthal wrote their names next to CLOTHING CLOSET and went down through the list.

Robert's neck started to itch when Mrs. Bernthal pointed to SNAKE.

Robert had been the snake monitor and had taken care of Sally, the green ribbon snake, from the day she arrived. Mrs. Bernthal had given Sally to them for being the best class in the whole school. Robert loved Sally. Sally made a little S curve when Robert stroked her back.

"Me! Me!"

He looked around. Lester Willis was standing up and calling out, as usual. Susanne Lee Rodgers and Kevin Kransky also had their hands up.

8

What was going on? When Sally first came into the class, everyone said the snake was slimy. Some girls, like Melissa Thurm, even said it was disgusting. But Robert thought from the first moment he saw her that Sally was beautiful.

Month after month, when new monitors were appointed for the other jobs, nobody wanted to take care of Sally, so Robert kept doing it. He didn't mind. Now, suddenly, everyone was interested.

Susanne Lee was so bossy, she made Robert grind his teeth. She would probably make Sally grind hers, too, if snakes had any teeth.

Kevin Kransky was always biting his nails. Robert was afraid he'd have spit on his hands when he handled Sally. Yuck! Now that would be disgusting!

Lester had once been a bully, but he was better now. That probably because Robert once helped him with his reading without telling anyone. Still, Lester could play rough. What if he hurt Sally?

"Lester and Susanne Lee, you will be our new snake monitors," said Mrs. Bernthal, adding their names to the chart.

"Cool!" shouted Lester.

Robert slouched in his chair. Mrs. Bernthal continued to assign monitors until all the jobs were filled. Robert got to be one of the window monitors along with Joey Rizzo. It was O.K., but it wasn't like being snake monitor.

This day was sure off to a bad start.

The Bad Fairy

"Class, be sure to take home your math books tonight. Study pages 34 to 39. We're having a test tomorrow."

Robert groaned. Math was his worst subject, unless you counted sports. In sports, at least someone took pity on him now and then and chose him for a team, even if they knew he was no good.

Maybe he could get sick, like Paul, and stay home from school! Then he wouldn't have to take the math test. He could go over to Paul's house and catch whatever he had. But his mom and Paul's mom probably wouldn't go for that. Besides, Paul probably had tonsillitis. He'd had that before, and Paul's mom said then that it wasn't catching.

After math, Mrs. Bernthal asked the class to work quietly on their Explorers project.

Robert's diorama was almost done when he turned around suddenly and knocked over the jar of yellow paint.

"Robert!" scolded Susanne Lee. "Look what you did!" As if he didn't know without her telling him. Susanne Lee acted like he had ruined her diorama of Robert Peary arriving at the North Pole, but only one little spot of yellow had splashed on the snowy scene. His own diorama, on the other hand, was completely ruined. The whole scene of Balboa, on a cliff looking out over the Pacific Ocean, was covered in yellow paint.

He would have to do it all over again. Robert spent the rest of the afternoon cleaning yellow paint off the table, the brushes, the water jar, and himself. He tossed the diorama in the trash.

It was good to hear the bell ring at three o'clock.

When Robert got home, nobody was there except for Huckleberry.

"Hi, Huck," he said, closing the door behind him and dropping his backpack. This was one part of his day that was always good, when the big yellow lab ran to greet him, wagging his tail, slobbering kisses all over him. Robert fell to his knees to hug the dog.

"You're lucky," he said to his dog, "that you don't have to go to school. I had one terrible day today. And I'm starved." He marched into the kitchen, Huck prancing along beside him. Robert saw a note on the refrigerator door.

Rob —
At the office. Will be home at 4 to take you to Dr. Fargus.
Mom

Oh no! He had forgotten he had an appointment with the orthodontist.

On the last visit, Robert thought he was getting braces like Charlie's. His brother's braces were red, white, and blue and were kind of cool.

But Dr. Fargus had told Robert's mom that Robert was too young for regular braces. What he needed was a palate expander. That, he explained, was a little metal device that would be placed on the roof of Robert's mouth and be attached to his upper teeth with little wires. Each day Robert would have to fit a key into a hole in the metal piece and turn it once. Little by little, that would expand his palate, making more room for his permanent teeth to come in.

That didn't sound cool at all. It sounded like mouth torture. Robert helped himself to a carton of apple juice from the fridge and went outside to the backyard with Huck. He sat on the step by the back door while Huck raced around the yard, sniffing along the fence.

"Yeah, I know those squirrels drive you crazy," said Robert. "They come in the yard just to tease you and then they leave before you get here." Robert drank his juice as he watched Huck sniff frantically at the roots of the apple tree.

Finally, Huck came over and lay down at Robert's feet.

"Hey, Huck. Do you think it's possible that a bad fairy touched me with her wand this morning and now she won't leave me alone?"

Huck rolled over on his back.

"I guess you don't believe in fairies," Robert said, rubbing the dog's belly. But he wasn't sure about them himself. SOME-THING was giving him all this bad luck.

Mouth Torture

Robert sat in the chair in Dr. Fargus's office, staring at all the equipment around him. If he wasn't sitting there, he'd probably think all this stuff was cool. It looked like something out of a creepy science fiction movie.

"Open wide," said Dr. Fargus, leaning over him. Dr. Fargus wore a white coat and thick glasses, which made him look like a mad scientist. Robert dropped his mouth open. He felt the chair tilt back as Dr. Fargus pumped the pedal with his foot.

Dr. Fargus took a small metal piece from the tray next to the chair and put it in Robert's mouth. It felt cold against the roof of his mouth. Robert tried to swallow, but he couldn't.

"Smdffssst," he said. That was supposed to be "I have to swallow," but he couldn't form the words with his mouth wide open and a metal contraption in the way. Dr. Fargus hung a long tube with a bent top over his lower teeth.

"I'll be done in a minute," said Dr. Fargus. "This drain will take care of the excess saliva that accumulates." The little tube sucked up Robert's spit with a slurping sound.

Dr. Fargus pushed and tapped and poked around in his mouth, stopping now and again to put one tool down and pick up another.

Robert wondered if Charlie had to go through all this to have his braces fitted,

and if he thought it was weird, too. He
stared at the wall with Dr. Fargus's certifi-
cates from dental school. He stared at the
chest with a gazillion drawers in it and
wondered what was in each one. He studied the light that was shining down on him.

He studied Dr. Fargus's face. The doctor
looked a little like Sir Mordred, the Black
Knight, in a horror movie Robert had seen

recently. He noticed that there were hairs growing in his nose.

"Ah, that's a good fit," Dr. Fargus said, finally, as he stood up. He removed the sucking tube. "Close your mouth slowly and see how that feels."

It felt as though there was a big metal hockey puck stuck on the roof of his mouth. He ran his tongue over it and around the wires that held the piece onto his teeth on both sides.

"How does that feel?" asked Dr. Fargus.

"It theels thlunnee," Robert said, as spit trickled down his chin.

"It will feel uncomfortable at first," said Dr. Fargus, handing him a tissue. "Your mouth will probably feel sore for two or three days, until you get used to it." He turned to Robert's mom. "You can give him Tylenol if he needs it," he said.

"Can he eat regular food?" asked his mom.

"Have him eat soft foods for the first few days," the doctor answered.

Robert felt like he wasn't even in the room as his mom and the doctor talked to each other over him.

"He will also have some trouble speaking . . . ," said Dr. Fargus.

No kidding, thought Robert.

"Until he's used to having the palate expander in his mouth," the doctor continued. "But he will get used to it, and that will improve over time."

Wrong! He would NEVER get used to it, Robert decided.

Dr. Fargus smiled. "That's it, young man. You're done." He pumped the chair upright, and Robert slid out. He kept his mouth closed tight. He was not going to make a fool of himself drooling again in front of Dr. Fargus and his mom.

Dr. Fargus pulled a sheet of paper off his desk in the next room and handed it to

Robert's mom. "This will explain about eating and speaking and cleaning the palate expander." He put his arm around Robert's shoulders as he walked them out the door.

"So," said Dr. Fargus, "you're on your way to having nice, straight permanent teeth. Doesn't that sound good?"

Robert just grunted. Right now, crooked teeth didn't sound half bad. In Robert's mind, Dr. Fargus had become the evil Sir Mordred, and his office was the torture chamber in an ancient dungeon.

Baby Food

Robert sat on his beanbag chair, picking at a scab on his elbow. His mouth was sore, and his tongue was tired from feeling around the metal piece and the wires all day. He couldn't help it. He wished he could pry the thing off, but it was cemented in.

"Rob, dinner's ready," called his mom from downstairs.

Rats. He had forgotten about dinner. Suddenly, the thought of food made him realize how hungry he was. He got up and went downstairs, *thump, thump, thump.* On his plate he saw three little piles. Robert had forgotten Dr. Fargus had said he wouldn't be able to chew anything at first, so he'd have to eat soft food.

His mom had given him cottage cheese, mashed potatoes with gravy, and carrots that she had put through the blender.

"That looks like baby food," said Charlie.

Robert stared into his plate. He tried to ignore his brother, who loved to tease him. He took a spoonful of cottage cheese.

It tasted all right, but it got stuck around the wires. He used his tongue to get it loose.

Robert didn't look up, but he just knew Charlie was waiting for an opportunity to laugh at him. He stabbed his fork into the mountain of mashed potatoes.

"So how is it going, Tiger?" asked his dad. Looking up, Robert forgot and started to answer, but when he opened his mouth to speak, he drooled. He quickly wiped his mouth with his napkin, but Charlie had seen it and was howling with laughter.

"Charlie, that's enough!" said Robert's mom, but Charlie didn't stop.

"Charlie, leave the table," commanded his dad.

Charlie left, but he was still shaking with laughter.

Robert wished he could disappear under the mound of mashed potatoes. "May I be ethcused?" he asked, slowly and carefully, so he didn't dribble down his chin. His mom looked at him sympathetically.

"Yes, you may," she said.

Robert slid off his chair and ran upstairs, Huckleberry at his heels. He closed the door to his room and flopped down on his bed, sniffling quietly into his pillow. Huckleberry leaped up next to him and licked Robert's ear. Robert couldn't hold it in any longer and cried, burying his face in Huckleberry's fur.

Paul had once said everyone had a rotten day now and then, when a lot of things seemed to go wrong, but once in a while a person could have a streak of bad things happen and it could be a double rotten day. Well, this was even worse than that. It was a triple rotten day. Maybe it would even go in the *Guinness Book of World Records.*

He got up and went to the telephone on the upstairs landing. He had to talk to Paul.

"Hello?" It was Paul's mom.

"Hi, Mithith Felcher. It'th Robert. Can I thpeak to Paul, pleathe?" Oops. He should have said "may I."

"Oh, Robert, I know Paul would love to talk to you, but his throat is so sore, I don't think he should talk at all."

"Oh," said Robert. "O.K." He hoped he didn't sound too disappointed.

"I'll tell Paul you called," said Mrs. Felcher.

"Thankth," said Robert. He hung up the phone and went back to his room.

Now he was having a triple rotten day and he couldn't even tell his best friend about it.

Loose Wire

The next day, Paul was still not back in school. Robert sat alone at lunch. He didn't want anyone else to see him drooling or eating baby food.

He opened his brown lunch bag and pulled out a plastic container instead of a sandwich baggie. It was yogurt. Strawberry yogurt. It tasted all right, but Robert wished he had a regular old salami sandwich like the ones he was used to. There were no cookies in the bag—just a nice, soft banana. Charlie was right. He was eating baby food.

After washing everything down with milk, Robert felt around inside his mouth with his tongue. Dr. Fargus had told him not to play around with the device, to try to keep his tongue off it. How could he do that? His tongue wouldn't stay still.

He emptied his tray into the trash barrel and went outside. Some kids were playing ball in the school yard, others were talking. Robert didn't feel like doing either. He went back inside and upstairs to his classroom. Mrs. Bernthal had given him permission to go up to the classroom by himself on his lunch hour to work on the class library.

The room was empty and quiet. Robert walked over to the bookcases that made up the classroom library and started to straighten up the books. He glanced over at Sally's tank, sitting on top of the supply cabinets.

Robert walked over and took the top off Sally's tank. "Hi," he said. He reached in and gently stroked her beautiful green body. Sally squiggled into an S curve. Robert didn't have to say a word. Sally was happy, and Robert was happy just being there with Sally again.

He knew it would sound silly to anyone else, but Robert believed Sally understood when he felt sad or lonely or happy. She was his third best friend. Paul was his first, Huck was his second, and Sally was his third. Robert kept that to himself.

Robert stayed with Sally, stroking her now and then, until the class and Mrs. Bernthal came back.

"Hey, what are you doing here?" said Lester, coming over to the snake tank.

"Nothing," said Robert.

"Well, you're not the monitor anymore," said Lester. "We get to take care of her now."

Robert swallowed hard. That's what he'd been afraid of.

During Silent Reading, Robert could hardly concentrate on the story in his book. He caught himself several times rolling his tongue around in his mouth.

Wait. Something felt different. One of the wires seemed to be a little loose. His mom would not be happy about that. Now his tongue was going crazy, feeling around that loose wire.

At last, school was over. He had one tired tongue. All day, he had struggled with making his tongue behave, but he just couldn't help himself. The wire was even looser by the end of the day.

Robert let himself into the house with his key, because no one was home except

Huckleberry. The big yellow dog greeted him, as always, with a wildly wagging tail.

In the kitchen, Robert found another Post-it on the fridge.

Rob—
Doing errands.
Back around 3:30.
Mom

Robert looked in the fridge and found pudding cups. Butterscotch—his favorite. He flopped on the sofa in the living room to eat his snack. Huckleberry curled up at his feet.

Robert tried not to wiggle the loose wire anymore, but with the last spoonful of pudding, he felt it come off. He took out the wire, brought it to the kitchen, and rinsed it off.

Back in the living room, he put it on the coffee table to show his mom.

What would she do? He'd know soon enough, when she came home.

"Come on, boy," he called to Huck, picking up a tennis ball. "Let's play some catch." Huck followed him out the back door and into the yard.

This was the best part of the day. School was over, and Robert could play with Huck. They both ran around the yard, throwing the ball and catching it, chasing each other, wrestling in the grass.

Huck ran to a corner of the yard and started digging.

"Give up, Huck," said Robert. "There's no squirrel there. It's just the smell of a squirrel."

Huck looked up at him, dirt on his nose, then went back to digging some more, dirt flying everywhere. Suddenly, he grabbed something and ran over to Robert with it.

"Yuck!" said Robert. "That's gross." It was a bone covered with yucky stuff. When they went into the house, Robert made Huck leave the bone outside. The dog bounded into the living room.

"Wait!" called Robert, but it was too late. Huck had tracked mud in from all that digging.

Robert grabbed Huck by the collar and led him to the kitchen, where he filled a basin with water and washed the rest of the mud off Huck's paws.

The living room was still a mess, and his mom would be home any minute. He pulled the hand vacuum cleaner off the wall in the broom closet and cleaned up the best he could.

He had just put the vacuum cleaner away when his mom came in.

"Hi, Robbie," she said.

"Hi, Mom."

"Was today any better?" she asked.

Robert had almost forgotten. Playing with Huck, he had not even thought about the metal piece in his mouth, or the broken wire!

"It was O.K. But . . . um . . . a wire came loose," he said.

"Really?" His mother sounded worried. "Is it just loose or did it come out?"

"It was loose first," he said, "and then it came off." He didn't mention that he was wiggling it with his tongue all day.

"Where is it?" his mom asked.

"I put it on the coffee table," he said. He went over to the table to show her. Huck was standing there.

The wire was gone.

Robert got down on his hands and knees and searched the carpet. Huck

thought he was playing and came close, to nuzzle Robert.

"No, Huck," Robert said. "Not now." He turned around. "Mom, it was here. Honest. It's not here now."

His mom looked worried. "Are you sure you didn't swallow it?"

"What? No, I'm sure. It came out," he said. "I washed it off and put it on the coffee table."

Robert saw his mom's expression change as she looked at Huckleberry. Robert knew right away what his mom was thinking. Huck was right where the wire had been. Could he have eaten it? Robert felt as though someone had hit him in the stomach.

"What'll we do?" he asked in a squeaky voice.

"I'll call the vet," his mom said, going to the telephone.

A minute later, she was whisking them both out the door and into her car. "We have to take him in right away, for an X-ray," she explained. "If he swallowed it, it will show up. And if it didn't get to his stomach yet, they can get it out with a scope."

"What's a scope?" Robert was beginning to panic.

"It's something they can put down his throat to find it and pull it out before it goes into his intestine, where it could get caught."

"Won't that hurt?" he asked.

"No," said his mom, easing the car out of the driveway. "They'll give him something to put him out first," said his mom. "He won't feel a thing."

Emergency!

At the vet's office, Huck wagged his tail as Dr. Treat came out to greet him.

"Don't worry," he said. "This should be quick." Dr. Treat took Huck to the back. Robert wished he could follow him, but he had to stay with his mom in the waiting room.

As he and his mom waited, Robert thought about his triple rotten day. It was now two days. Did it have a new name when it went into a second day? He must be nearing a record now.

About twenty minutes later, Dr. Treat came out with Huck walking slowly behind him. "You have nothing to worry about," he said. "Huckleberry didn't swallow anything he shouldn't have. He's still drowsy from the medication, but he'll be fine in a few minutes."

Robert knelt down on the floor and gave Huck a big hug, even if Huck was still too groggy to appreciate it.

"Next we have to see Dr. Fargus," said Robert's mom.

Now that Huckleberry was O.K., his mom was back on track.

They got in the car, with Huckleberry in the backseat. Huck loved the car. He was awake now, and already had his head out the window. Robert wished they could just go home and play.

"Mom, do I really have to do this?" asked Robert.

"Yes, I'm afraid so," said his mom. "Don't you want strong, straight teeth?"

"I guess so," said Robert, who really hadn't thought much about his teeth. He knew he had to brush and floss to keep his teeth healthy, and he didn't mind that—he did that all the time. But this . . . this . . . mouth torture was something else.

"But what if Huck had swallowed the wire? Or if I had? It can be dangerous."

"You have a point," said his mom, "and I plan to speak to Dr. Fargus about that. I'd like him to explain to me how we can prevent this from happening again."

"Are you mad at me for making the wire come out?" asked Robert.

His mom smiled. "No, I'm not mad at you, Robbie," she said. "Asking you not to wiggle your tongue around the palate expander is like asking you not to think of elephants."

"What do you mean?"

"Well, what happens when I say 'Don't think about elephants'?"

"Um . . . I . . . think about elephants," said Robert.

"The minute your attention is called to something, it's in your mind, right on the surface. You can't NOT think of it," his mom said.

Robert smiled. "That's cool."

"Well, you probably would have wiggled the wire, anyway," said his mom. "It's human nature to be curious, especially when something is not the way it usually is."

Robert was relieved that his mom understood. But would Dr. Fargus?

A Mess

Robert climbed into the orthodontist's chair once again.

Dr. Fargus wasn't upset. He talked to Robert as he removed the palate expander from his mouth. It took some tapping to loosen it, but that wasn't bad.

"I'm sorry this has been so uncomfortable for you," he said. He sounded like he meant it.

"Aaa ooo," said Robert, his mouth wide.

Dr. Fargus held up the palate expander.

"You get a break, young man, while I order a new one," he said.

Robert smiled at being called a young man. It made him feel good.

Dr. Fargus motioned for Robert to get down from the chair. "I'll call you when it's ready," he said to Robert's mom. He looked at Robert again. "Meanwhile, you can eat anything you like."

"Yes!" said Robert, visions of hamburgers floating in his head.

He didn't even have to tell his mom. On the way home, they stopped at the store to pick up hamburger meat and his favorite chocolate-covered jelly cookies. She also bought salami for his lunch.

"Rob, I'm still wondering what happened to that wire," said his mom as they drove the rest of the way home. "If it's around, there's still the possibility that Huck will find it and swallow it."

Robert searched his brain for ideas about where the wire could be. He had checked his pockets and the carpet around the table where the wire had been. He even checked where he had cleaned up Huck's muddy footprints.

The footprints! Of course!

"Mom!"

"What is it?"

"I know where the wire is."

"Really? Where?"

Robert told his mom about the digging and the yucky bone and the muddy footprints and using the hand vacuum cleaner. "I bet Huck brushed the wire onto the floor with his tail, and I vacuumed it up by mistake."

"There's only one way to find out," said his mom, laughing.

When they got home, Robert grabbed the hand vacuum cleaner and was opening it when his mom said, "Better take that outside."

It was a tiny bit too late. Dirt flew out. Robert clamped it back together and took it out to the backyard. Huck followed him. A moment later, his mom came after them.

"Here," she said, handing him some newspapers and a pair of rubber gloves. "These will help."

Robert slowly opened the vacuum cleaner over the newspaper. Even though most of the dirt fell out on the newspaper, dust flew into the air. Huck sneezed and backed away.

Robert pulled on the rubber gloves. Bit by bit, he sifted through the dirt, looking for the wire, which was no bigger than a

paper clip. The rubber gloves did help, but what he needed was a clothespin for his nose!

"Here it is!" he shouted at last.

His mom came out to see. "Good work, Rob," she said. She took the wire from him. "I'll put this in a safe place. Meanwhile, clean up this mess before your father gets home."

Robert rolled up the newspaper and put it in the trash. He rinsed off the rubber gloves and left them by the sink to dry.

His mom looked pleased. "You solved the mystery of the missing wire. You'd make a good detective."

"Maybe," Robert answered, "but I'd rather be an orthodontist."

"Really?" said his mom. "I thought you wanted to work with animals."

"I do. But I want to be like Dr. Fargus. Do you think animals need palate expanders or retainers?" Robert pictured him opening Huck's mouth to examine him for a palate expander.

Robert's mom laughed. "I don't know. That's an interesting idea."

Robert laughed, too. Sometimes he cracked himself up.

Hamburger Again

Dinner was late because of all the excitement, but Robert didn't mind. They were having hamburgers. He drooled, but this time it was for the juicy burger on his plate.

"Robert, for the next few days, while you can still eat normally, we'll eat your favorite foods."

"Even takeout?" he asked.

"Even takeout," said his mom.

"Cool!" said Charlie, giving Robert a high five. Sometimes Robert and Charlie saw eye to eye on things. They both knew

51

their mom was not a great cook, and take-out meant they didn't have to eat her cooking.

"Mom?"

"Yes, Rob?"

"I decided the palate expander is probably a good thing, once you get past the drooling and stuff."

His mom looked surprised. "I'm glad to hear it, Rob. But what makes you say that?"

"Dr. Fargus told me he was going to invent a better palate expander one day so kids could eat hamburgers and other good stuff without a problem."

"Ah," said Robert's mom. "That would be good."

"Yeah." Robert smiled.

BAM! Something made a loud pop in the kitchen.

Robert's mom jumped up and ran to the oven. She opened the door, and lots of smoke billowed out.

"Oh no!" she exclaimed.

"What happened?" asked Mr. Dorfman, who had run in after her.

"My apple pie," said Robert's mom. "It exploded!"

Robert looked at Charlie, and Charlie looked at Robert. They couldn't help it— they both burst out laughing.

"It isn't funny!" their mom wailed. "I thought it would be nice to have apple pie with dinner tonight, in honor of Rob's being able to eat real food again."

Robert tried to stop laughing. That was really nice of his mom. But everyone knew about her cooking. Maybe it was just as well it exploded.

Huck went over to the oven, sniffing.

"Well, I guess Huckleberry will have what's left of the pie."

"See? You've made someone very happy with your pie," said Robert's dad.

Mrs. Dorfman had a strange look on her face. Robert and Charlie snickered again.

"Mom, didn't you buy some chocolate-covered jelly cookies today?" asked Robert.

"Yes, I did. . . ."

"Then we can have those for dessert," said Robert, jumping up to get them.

"Yeah," said Charlie. "Everyone likes chocolate-covered jelly cookies. Right, Dad?"

Mr. Dorfman nodded.

"The boy has a good point," said Mr. Dorfman.

"And it isn't like we're starving," said Robert. His mom always made him feel good about his disasters. Maybe he could help her now, with hers.

"You're all being very nice," said Robert's mom, returning to the table with the coffeepot. She poured a cup for Robert's dad and another for herself. "Tomorrow, we'll have apple pie for dessert, I promise."

Charlie let out a groan. Robert kicked him under the table. He hoped his mom didn't hear it.

"I'll pick one up from the bakery," his mom added.

"Great!" they all answered at once.

After dinner, Robert went upstairs to his room to do his homework. Huck was there at his side.

"Hey," said Robert, patting the dog. "I get to choose what we have for dinner tomorrow night, and I choose pepperoni pizza." Huck danced around and found one of his toys, swinging it from his mouth, jawing it so the squeaker squeaked.

"Huck, you know what I think?"

Huckleberry stopping swinging the goose and stood there staring up at Robert.

"I think my triple rotten day is over."

Paul's Back

Robert sprang out of bed next morning, three minutes before the alarm was set to go off.

"Yes!" he said, shutting off the alarm button.

Sure enough, Paul was back on his corner when Robert got there.

"Boy, am I glad to see you!" said Robert, running up to him, his backpack bouncing.

"Yeah! Me, too," said Paul. He picked up his backpack from the sidewalk. "It was beginning to be a little boring. No, a LOT boring."

"I'm talking about worse than boring," said Robert. "I'm talking about a bad day, rotten luck, a horrible, no good, hope-it-never-happens-again streak of bad things happening."

"Really? What happened?"

Robert told him. He started with that first morning when Charlie hogged the bathroom, then all the things that went wrong that day, including having the palate expander put in, and on through the next day, when the wire came loose and he lost it and they thought Huck had swallowed it. He told him about the X-ray, and Dr. Fargus, and his sore mouth. He told Paul how he tried to call him, but his mom said Paul's throat was sore and he couldn't talk.

"I'm sorry," said Paul.

"That's O.K.," said Robert. "I know you were sick. It's just that it was a triple rotten day, and I didn't have anyone to talk to about it." He walked along with new energy in every step. "I thought I'd make a new record and get in the *Guinness Book of World Records,*" he finished.

"I don't think you had a triple rotten day," said Paul finally.

"Really?" Robert slowed down a bit. He couldn't imagine why not. It seemed terrible at the time. Maybe being out sick was worse? How could he be so dumb? He hadn't even asked Paul how he felt.

"Oh. Hey. How are you feeling?" he asked.

"I'm fine," said Paul. "Thanks. I think you had more than a triple rotten day," he added.

"Really?" What could be worse than a triple rotten day? Robert was amazed. Maybe he made a record after all.

Paul nodded. Then he said, "Well, to start with, it was not a day, it was two days. But then—think about it. You thought Huck had swallowed a wire, but found out he was O.K. That was good."

Robert let that sink in.

"Then, the wire came loose, but it made Dr. Fargus get you a new, better palate expander."

Robert hadn't seen it that way, but Paul was right. That was also a good thing.

"And finally," said Paul, "the evil Sir Mordred the Black Knight turned into your hero."

Robert sighed. Paul could always see things in a way that made him feel better.

"It was kind of neat there for a while, thinking of getting into the *Guinness Book of World Records,*" said Robert.

"If you're going to get in the *Guinness Book of World Records,*" said Paul, "you ought to pick something that's more fun than having bad luck."

"Yeah. Like having the most dogs," said Robert.

"Or drawing the most pictures," said Paul.

"Or eating the most chocolate-covered jelly cookies," said Robert.

"Or riding a bike the longest," said Paul.

It was so good to have Paul back. The walk to school had been so long and boring without him.

In the classroom, Robert saw Susanne Lee and Lester at Sally's tank.

"Oh, yeah," he said to Paul as they put their backpacks at their table. "Mrs. Bernthal chose new monitors. Sally got Susanne Lee and Lester."

Paul spun around. "No way!" he said.

"Way," said Robert. He couldn't resist going over for a look. Paul followed him.

"Hello, Robert," said Susanne Lee sweetly. "Have you come to see your girl-friend?"

What made Susanne Lee such a jerk? Everyone knew she was the smartest one in the class. But did she always have to act like she owned everything?

"I just came to see if Sally is still alive," said Robert. "I figure she might have died of fright when you came near her."

"You're pitiful," Susanne Lee said and walked off toward her desk, her hair bouncing. Robert didn't care. She made him mad sometimes.

"What's that in Sally's tank?" asked Paul.

It was a big rock.

Lester came over. "Yo, Rob," he said.

"Who put that rock in there?" asked Robert.

"I did," said Lester. "It's a hot rock. We got it so Sally would always be warm. You know how bad cold is for snakes."

"Cool," said Robert. He had seen hot rocks at the pet store. He smiled as he remembered the scary time Sally got loose over a cold winter weekend. He had thought she might die, but the custodian saw her and brought her down to the boiler room to keep warm.

"That's a good idea," Robert said, touching the hot rock with his finger. Maybe Lester wasn't such a bad snake monitor after all.

"Susanne Lee bought it," Lester added.

Susanne Lee? Robert couldn't believe it. As he and Paul walked back to their table, he thought about what he'd said to Susanne Lee. He knew he ought to apologize.

"I'll be right back," he said to Paul. He walked over to Susanne Lee at the next table. "That was nice," he said finally.

Susanne Lee looked around at him.

"The hot rock for Sally," he said.

"Thanks," she said. There was a pause. "You're not the only one who likes Sally, you know."

Robert's neck itched. He felt his cheeks get hot. "Yeah. I didn't know." He went back to his table and sat down.

Things sure had a way of working out in the most unexpected ways. Or was it that Robert had figured out how to make them work?

Deciding to give the palate expander a chance—that was his idea. Learning to trust Susanne Lee and Lester to take care of Sally—that was hard, but he had to do it. Finding a way to solve problems was something he could do.

Maybe he would be an orthodontist only part of the time, and a vet another part of the time. With the rest of the time, he could be someone who solved problems or crimes, like a detective.

This was a peculiar day. After the last two days, it seemed to fly by.

When school was over, Robert and Paul started the long walk home.

"I've been thinking," said Paul. "What about trying the most flavors of ice cream?"

"You mean for getting into the *Guinness Book of World Records*?" asked Robert.

Paul nodded. "My mom always has ice cream around because of my tonsillitis. She says it's good for my throat. We could start there."

"O.K.," said Robert. "I have to eat soft food when I get my new palate expander. Ice cream is soft. I can ask for a different flavor every night."

"Cool."

"I once had banana cinnamon swirl," said Robert.

"I had mango," answered Paul.

"I have to call my mother to tell her I'm at your house."

"Yeah."

They ran the rest of the way to Paul's house, eager to get started.

Wonder Dogs

"It's a perfect day for shopping," said Robert's mom the next morning. It was Saturday, and Robert and Paul were moping around Robert's house because they couldn't ride their bikes.

"Can you take us to the mall with you?" asked Robert.

"Sure," said his mom. "What do you want at the mall?"

"I need pet food," he answered. "And Paul needs a glitter pen from the hobby shop. Right, Paul?"

Paul nodded. He loved going to the hobby shop, with all its art supplies. Robert didn't need much of an excuse to go to the pet store, either. He loved seeing the animals, and the owner let him spend time with them.

"I guess so, then," said Robert's mom.

They listened to their instructions as Robert's mom dropped them at the stretch of mall where the hobby and pet shops were.

"At twelve o'clock sharp, meet me at the west entrance where we came in," she told them.

The boys scampered to the hobby shop first. After they looked at all the models and art supplies, Paul bought a green glitter pen, and they went two doors down to the pet store.

A video display caught Robert's attention.

"Did you see that?" he asked Paul.

"Wow!" was all Paul could say.

They had just seen a golden retriever jump through a flaming hoop, crawl through a tunnel, and leap over a fence to get to its master. Now, the dog climbed steps and jumped over barrels in an amazing obstacle course.

"May I help you, boys?" asked a saleswoman.

The video continued playing on the pet store's TV set, high above dog supplies on the back wall.

"Um, I need this," said Robert, holding out a big rawhide bone he had picked out earlier. The video had caught his eye and stopped him on his way to the checkout counter.

"Right over there," said the saleswoman, pointing. The badge on her shirt read *Hi! My name is Nina.*

"Thank you . . . ," he said. He almost said

"Thank you, Nina," but his mom had told him not to call grownups by their first names and he didn't know her last one.

As Robert paid for the rawhide bone and waited for his change, he whispered to Paul. "Look, that's the video we were watching." In a bin by the front door was a stack of videos. Over it was a sign that read: Jeff Roman's Wonder Dogs—On Sale—$9.99.

Paul went over and picked one up. He came back to Robert reading the copy off the box. "'Dog handler Jeff Roman shows how you can turn your ordinary dog into a wonder dog who can brave unusual and complicated obstacles in a masterful display of trust, loyalty, and obedience. . . .'"

Robert listened as he took his change and his package from the clerk.

"I bet I could teach Huckleberry to do some of those things," said Robert.

"Jump through a hoop of fire?" asked Paul, his eyes wide.

"No, maybe not the fire thing," said Robert, looking at his change. "My mom is really strict about playing with fire. But Huck could go through a tunnel." He counted four dollars and thirty-seven cents left. "I could build one myself in the backyard. We don't even need the video."

"Uh-oh," said Paul, remembering their last attempt to build something. When Paul had run for class president, they heard that candidates needed a platform. They didn't know that meant a plan for what Paul would do if he was elected. So they built a wooden platform out of old lumber in Paul's backyard.

"I know what you're thinking," said Robert, "but this doesn't take that kind of building. I need to find tubes that Huck can

71

crawl through. Then I have to connect them with tape or something."

"What kind of tubes?" asked Paul.

"I don't know. I haven't figured out that part yet," said Robert. "Is it time to meet my mom yet?"

Paul looked at his watch. "It's twenty minutes to twelve," he said. "She said to meet her at twelve o'clock at the west entrance."

They walked past a few windows and stopped at the Computers 4 U store.

"We have a few minutes. Let's go in," said Paul.

"O.K." Robert followed him in.

Paul went right over to the computers on display and started typing on one. Robert typed on the one next to it.

A salesclerk who looked like a teenager walked over. "Hi. My name is Corey. Are you interested in a new computer?" he asked.

Boy! Was he ever! All of them—his mom, his dad, his brother Charlie, and he—had to share his mom's old computer that she used for her business. "N . . . n . . . no," said Robert, moving away from the computer. Paul kept typing away at his.

"Why don't you take this home and show it to your mother?" the young clerk asked. He held out a flyer with *Sale! Sale! Sale!* written all over it. His mom liked sales. Robert took the flyer.

"Thanks . . . Corey," said Robert. It seemed O.K. this time to call the salesclerk by name. After all, Corey wasn't quite a grownup yet, and he had practically asked to be called by his first name.

Paul checked his watch. "Uh-oh. Now we're going to be late. We'd better run!"

Robert ran after Paul down the mall corridor to the west entrance. The good smells from the food court one level up were drifting down and following them. There was his mom, waiting at the doors.

"Come on, boys. Shake a leg," she said.

Paul laughed, but Robert was used to hearing his mom say that when she tried to hurry him and Charlie along.

Robert rolled up the flyer from the computer store and stuck it in his back pocket. He'd show it to his mom later. Right now, all he could think about was food.

Obstacle Course

As they pulled into the driveway, Robert could see Huckleberry's face in the window. Robert and Paul unbuckled their seat belts and jumped out. No sooner had they gone into the house than they were out again in the backyard with Huckleberry. The big yellow dog ran around the yard, looking for squirrels. Robert looked around. How could he make an obstacle course in the backyard?

"There's nothing here but lawn chairs," he said.

"So let's use those," said Paul.

Robert picked up one of the chairs and placed it in the center of the yard, upside down. Paul dragged over another one, turning it over and placing it end to end with the first one.

"You think Huck can jump over these?" asked Paul.

"Sure," said Robert. He coaxed Huck to come to him. Huck went around the chairs and up to Robert.

"No, Huck, jump over the chairs!" said Robert. He took Huck by the collar and led him back to the other side of the chairs. Each time Robert said "Jump!" Huck walked around the chairs instead of jumping over them.

"Wait," said Robert. "I have an idea."

He went into the house and came out with dog biscuits in his pocket. Then he took Huck by the collar and said, "Sit!"

Huck knew how to do that, and he sat. "Stay!"

Huck knew that, too, but he looked like he might jump up at any moment. Robert reinforced the command by giving him the hand signal for "stay" with his palm facing the dog. Huck stayed as Robert went around the chairs to the opposite side. Robert kept one palm still facing Huck for the "stay" command and held up a biscuit in his other. Huck's eyes were alert, but his drooling tongue told them he was thinking of that dog biscuit.

"Jump!" said Robert.

Huck jumped over the chairs. Robert gave him the biscuit, and Huck devoured it. His tail wagged happily.

They did it again and again until Huck got it down pat. Finally, they took the third lawn chair and put it on top of the other

79

two. Robert made Huck stay on one side and walked around to the other.

"This looks hard," said Paul, sizing up the situation. "Do you think he can do it?"

"I don't know," said Robert. "Ready?"

"Ready," Paul answered.

Robert held up another biscuit. Huck drooled.

"Jump!" called Robert.

Without a moment's hesitation, Huck leaped over the stack of chairs, clearing them completely.

"Good dog!" shouted Paul.

Robert got down on his knees and hugged Huck. "Good boy!" he said, over and over again.

After their first afternoon of wonder-dog training, Paul had to go home.

"Do you think Huck can be a wonder dog?" asked Robert.

"He looked pretty good today," said Paul. "We'd better come up with more obstacles, though, or he'll be more of a one-wonder dog."

Robert broke up laughing. "I know one trick I'd like to teach him," he said.

"What's that?" asked Paul, picking up his backpack.

"How to do our homework."

They cracked up all over again.

After dinner, Robert took out his homework assignment. By Friday, he had to write a report about something important that happened in the state of New Jersey. He could find out online. Charlie had showed him how to use a search engine to find information when he was doing homework. Robert took a paper and pencil with him and went down the hall to the spare bedroom that his mom had turned into her office at home, and where she had her computer.

There was a sound coming from the room. He thought his mom was downstairs making dinner. He didn't know she was using the computer. He went up to the door and looked in. Charlie was at the keyboard.

"Yo, bro!" said Charlie. "Come on in. You're just in time to see Bruce the Warrior go through the Cave of Catastrophe. I've got to help him get out and to the Forgotten Fields, or he's doomed!"

Robert watched for a few seconds over Charlie's shoulders. Then he said, "I have to look something up for homework."

"Man, I can't stop now," said Charlie. "Come back later."

"But I want to do it now so I can finish this report."

"I can't stop now. I'm winning."

"Charlie . . ."

"Go away! I got here first. You can search later."

"But you're not doing schoolwork. Mom said . . ."

"Mom said. Mom said. You're such a baby. Go on, tell Mom. I double dare you."

Robert knew he couldn't tell on his brother, not on a double dare. Frustrated, he went back to his room. He would just have to wait to use the computer.

As Robert sat down to dinner, he unrolled the flyer from the computer store and put it near his mom's plate.

"What's this?" she said, sitting down.

"It's a sale," said Robert.

"A sale on what?" his mom asked.

"Computers."

"Oh," she said, laughing. "Computers." She handed the bowl of mashed potatoes to him. "That's nice."

Robert knew from the way she laughed she wasn't taking it seriously. He took the bowl of mashed potatoes and put a big spoonful onto his plate. Robert didn't press the issue. He had promised not to ask for anything else after he got what he wanted more than anything—a dog, Huckleberry.

Robert looked over at Huck on his doggy mat, napping while they ate dinner. He'd rather have Huck than a computer any old time.

E-mail Buddies

Tap, tap, tap. "May I have your undivided attention, please?" asked Mrs. Bernthal, tapping her ruler on the desk. Mrs. Bernthal talked to the class as though they were adults.

"We have been asked to take part in a very interesting program that fits right in with our study of the fifty states. As you know, we started with our own state of New Jersey."

Robert added a mustache to the picture of Sponge Bob on his notebook cover as he listened.

"A computer company has offered to match up children in our class with a third grade class in another state," Mrs. Bernthal announced.

"Which one?" Lester Willis called out. "I have a cousin in Indiana."

"Thank you, Lester."

"My Aunt Jen lives in New York City," said Elizabeth Street.

"My grandma lives in Florida," said Robert.

Oops! Mrs. Bernthal frowned. She didn't like it when they called out instead of raising their hands. Robert had forgotten.

"As I was saying," she said, "the computer company will choose the state for us, and match us up with another third grade class there. You will each have your own e-mail buddy, and you'll write to him or her every week."

Him or her? Could his e-mail buddy turn out to be a girl? Robert hadn't thought of that. What if she was like Susanne Lee Rodgers? His neck got itchy just thinking about it.

Vanessa Nicolini raised her hand.

"Yes, Vanessa?" Mrs. Bernthal said, smiling.

"What will we write about?"

Robert was glad Vanessa had asked that question. He was worried about it, too.

"Write about yourself and what you like to do," said Mrs. Bernthal. "Or write about your family, your pets, your school, your community."

"And about New Jersey!" shouted Lester.

Mrs. Bernthal sighed. "Yes," she said. "And about New Jersey. You should know quite a lot about New Jersey by Friday." She pulled down the map of the United States.

"Lester, please show us where New Jersey is," said Mrs. Bernthal. He bounded up and took the pointer.

Lester looked at the map. The class snickered. He had the pointer on Montana and let it slide over Nebraska and down to Kansas and Oklahoma before Mrs. Bernthal stopped him.

"Emily, can you show us, please?"

Emily Asher went up and immediately put the pointer tip on New Jersey, all the way over to the right.

"Tonight for homework you're each getting a map of the United States. You are to fill in the names of each of the states. Your e-mail buddies might be from any one of the other states, so I want you to know where they are."

"I will also send you home with a form to fill out. If you would like to be part of the program, complete the form and bring it back tomorrow. The children in the other class will be doing the same. When all the information is in, it will be put into the computer, and then the computer will match you with someone who has the same general interests as you. Do you wish to participate?"

"Yes!" they answered enthusiastically.

"Good," said Mrs. Bernthal. "I think we'll all learn a great deal."

Kristi Mills helped hand out the maps. Robert found Florida on his right away. His grandma had sent him a key chain once, in the shape of the state. He wondered which one was Wyoming. He knew that lots of dinosaur bones were found there.

When the class went to the Media Center later that morning, Robert had to wait again to use a computer for his report on New Jersey. Kevin Kransky, Susanne Lee, Emily, Vanessa, and Kristi had gotten to them first. Robert went to the encyclopedia and looked up New Jersey. He copied down the natural resources and major products of the state. He noted the capital was Trenton and that the major rivers were the Delaware and the Hudson. More than 8 million people lived in New Jersey.

It was almost twenty-five minutes before a computer was free, and then he only had time to type in his question:

Search Were there dinosaurs in New Jersey?

To Robert's amazement, the first site he clicked on was about dinosaur fossils, and he almost stopped breathing when he read: *The first dinosaur fossil found in the U.S. was a thigh bone found by Dr. Caspar Wistar, in Gloucester County, New Jersey, in 1787. (It has since been lost, but more fossils were later found in the area.)*

Yes! Robert slid to the edge of his chair. He barely had time to print out that information; it was time to leave.

Good grief! The first U.S. dinosaur fossils, right here in his state! That was definitely something interesting to write about. He'd have to try the computer at home again tonight.

The Hoop

"**A** Hula-Hoop? What's that?" asked Paul, running alongside Robert on the way home from school.

"It's something my parents used in the old days for fun. It's a big ring made out of plastic tubing, and if you wiggle your body just right you can get it to spin around you without falling down."

"Huh?"

"I'll have to show you," said Robert. "My mom had it down in the basement. She said I could use it for our obstacle course. But first she showed me how to do it. I'm not good at it, but my mom really is. You should see her."

"So what are you going to do with this Hula-Hoop?" asked Paul.

"I'll show you. Come on." Robert broke into a full run. When they got to his house, they practically exploded through the front door.

"Well, hello, boys," said Mrs. Dorfman.

"Hello, Mrs. Dorfman," said Paul, catching his breath.

"Hi, Mom," said Robert, patting an excited Huckleberry with one hand as he slid his backpack off. The two sank to the floor, Robert hugging Huck while Huck's tail beat a *thwap! thwap! thwap!* on the floor.

"And hi to you, pal," said Robert.

"What are you boys up to today, that you're in such a hurry?" asked Robert's mom.

"We're working on the obstacle course. We're going to teach Huck to jump through a hoop. Mom, can you show Paul how you do the Hula-Hoop?"

"Well . . . I guess so," replied Mrs. Dorfman. She looked around. "Where is it?"

"In my room. I'll get it." Robert ran upstairs and came back down with the orange plastic hoop.

Robert's mom took it and slipped it over her head. "Well, you start by putting the hoop around you. . . ." She brought the hoop down around her and held it with both hands. As she moved her hips from side to side and around, she let go with her hands. The hoop stayed up as long as she kept moving.

"That's cool," said Paul. Robert's mom stopped swinging her hips, and the hoop fell to the ground. She stepped out of it and picked it up.

94

"Here," she said, handing it to Paul. "Try it."

Paul moved every which way, but the hoop kept falling. "This is hard," he said.

"Not once you get the hang of it," said Robert's mom.

"Maybe we should just stick to using it for the obstacle course," said Robert.

"Yeah," said Paul. They went outside, Huck trailing after them.

Paul held the hoop upright just off the ground. Robert made Huck sit and stay on one side of it, just as they had done with the lawn chairs, and went around to the other side with a dog biscuit. He held up the biscuit.

"Jump!" he said.

Huck seemed to cower before he went around Paul and the hoop to Robert.

"It looked like it spooked him," said Robert, not sure what to do with the dog biscuit, since Huck hadn't actually done the trick. He put it back in his pocket.

They tried it again and again and again, but each time, Huck went around instead of through the hoop. Finally, Robert had an idea.

"Let's try hanging the hoop from the tree branch," he said. "Maybe he's afraid of it while you're holding it."

"Yeah, maybe it wobbled," said Paul.

They got the ladder and some rope out of the garage. Paul climbed up the apple tree with the rope, and Robert held the hoop up so Paul could reach it. Then Paul looped the rope around the hoop. He tied the rope to a branch of the tree. Robert was glad Paul didn't mind climbing, because he was nervous about heights.

Paul climbed down again, and they admired their cleverness.

"That looks good," said Robert.

"Now if only it works," said Paul.

They tried the trick again, but Huck just wouldn't jump through the hoop; he always ran around it. Robert even climbed through it to show Huck what to do, but still Huck wouldn't do it. Every now and then Huck left them completely to run after more imaginary squirrels.

They were exhausted. Robert gave Huck a biscuit, anyway. "That's enough for one day," said Robert.

"Yeah. Not every trick is going to be as easy as the lawn chairs," said Paul.

They went inside and up to Robert's room.

"Let's do our new words," said Robert.

"O.K.," Paul agreed.

Mrs. Bernthal gave them a new and difficult word to learn each day, to improve their vocabularies. So far this week she had given them *amphitheater, meticulous,* and *ambivalent.* She asked them to practice by putting the new words into a sentence.

Robert stretched out across the bed, and Paul sat in the beanbag chair. They wrote, and thought, and wrote some more.

"I got one," said Robert. "I am *ambivalent* about this homework."

Paul smiled. "That's good." He read from his notebook. "I am *ambivalent* about Huckleberry becoming a wonder dog. I like him the way he is."

"That's two sentences. Mrs. Bernthal said one sentence."

"O.K. Leave off the second part." Paul erased as Robert read another one.

"When my dog becomes a wonder dog, I will have him perform in an *amphitheater.*"

Paul nodded his approval. "How about this?" he asked. "I got a nosebleed sitting in the highest seat of the *amphitheater.*"

This cracked them up.

"Just one more," said Robert. "Hmmm. *Meticulous*. That should be easy."

They were quiet for a long time, scribbling one thing after another and scratching them out again.

"This is hard," said Robert.

"My homework is no longer *meticulous*," said Paul.

"That's it! You got it."

Paul smiled. "O.K. If you insist." He closed his notebook. "What's yours?"

"Hmmm," said Robert. He found the form they had to fill out for Mrs. Bernthal. "We have to be *meticulous* about filling this out," he said. "Are you going to have an e-mail buddy?"

"Yikes. I forgot about that," said Paul. "I'll do mine tonight. I have to get home now. Yeah, I'm doing it." He got up to leave. "Aren't you? It should be fun."

"Yeah, I'm doing it," said Robert. "I just

have to figure out how to write an e-mail without a computer."

"Oh, right. You can always use mine," said Paul. "See you tomorrow."

That night, Robert lay across his bed filling out the form. He wrote in his first name only. Mrs. Bernthal said that was for privacy. They were not to give out their addresses or telephone numbers, either. He filled in the name of his school, Clover Hill Elementary, and his town, River Edge. He had to give a preference for a girl or a boy buddy, and he chose "boy." He wasn't sure he'd know how to write to a girl. Under "hobbies and interests," he made a long list:

pet sitting
dinosaurs
bike riding
rock collecting
weird and wacky fact books
snowboarding

Robert read his list again. He wasn't sure snowboarding belonged there, because he'd only done it once, but he liked how it looked so he left it in.

Suddenly, Huck jumped up next to him and rolled over on his back. Robert was rubbing Huck's belly when he remembered to add

dog training

He got up. He heard Charlie moving around in his room. His mom had been downstairs reading in the living room when he saw her last. His dad was probably grading students' papers in the den. Now was a good time to try for the computer. Robert picked up his notebook and pencil and went up the hall to his mom's little office.

Click, click, click. Click, click, click. Oh no. His dad was sitting at the computer. It looked like he was doing the monthly accounting.

"Dad!" he exclaimed, not meaning to sound so surprised.

"Hey, Tiger," said his dad. "You want to get in here?"

"Um, well . . . I just have to look something up."

His dad got up and patted the chair. "Here you go. It's all yours," he said.

Robert sat down. He typed in his question. He pulled up the site about the first dinosaur bones in America and printed it out.

While the printer chugged away, he looked at the list of sites on his search results. There were several that mentioned the dinosaur fossils in New Jersey. Robert printed out one other one, but he couldn't do any more. His dad was hanging around, fiddling with papers, reading the calendar. It was making him nervous.

"Thanks, Dad," Robert said, collecting the pages he had printed.

"Sure thing, Tiger," said his dad.

If he was going to beat the computer hogs, he'd have to learn to be faster getting to the computer in school, get up before everyone else in the morning at home, or work at Paul's computer after school.

As he got into his pajamas that night, Robert made a promise to himself. When he grew up and had kids of his own, he would definitely get each kid his own dog and his own computer!

Ice Fishing

The class was buzzing when they came back from lunch. Word had gotten around that there was news about their e-mail buddies.

Mrs. Bernthal had pulled down the map of the United States. She pointed to a shape in the middle of the country, at the very top, where it touched Canada.

"Robert, please come up and read the name of this state," said Mrs. Bernthal.

Robert went up and stared at the word. It was long. He held his breath, then let it out and tried to say it. "Minn . . ." he said.

"Minn- Minnes- Minne-so-ta." Finally, he said it all at once. "Minnesota!"

"Thank you, Robert. Yes. Minnesota. That is the state we will be studying next. It's the state your e-mail buddies live in. Does anyone know anything about the state of Minnesota?"

"I think it's all farms," Kristi Mills said.

"What else?" asked Mrs. Bernthal.

"Cows," said someone.

"Chickens," said someone else.

"That's enough, class," said Mrs. Bernthal. "Only tell me what you know for sure."

"They have a football team called the Vikings," said Kevin.

"Yes, that's true. What else?" She pointed to a big lake at the top of the state.

Lester called out, "There's a lake!"

"Right. It's on Lake Superior—one of the Great Lakes."

"I went to a great lake last summer," said Joey Rizzo. "It was called Lake

Wittowattamee, in New Hampshire."
Several children giggled.

"It's cold because it's very far north,"
said Susanne Lee.

Robert wished he had said that. He had
just been thinking it.

"Tell you what," said Mrs. Bernthal,
putting down the pointer. "Instead of
guessing, let's see how much you can find
out about the state of Minnesota. And look
up the town of White Bear, which is where
your e-mail buddies go to school."

Robert tapped his pencil on his notebook. White Bear. White bears were polar
bears. Was it so cold in Minnesota that
they had polar bears?

Mrs. Bernthal gave them permission to continue working on their projects about the state of New Jersey, but asked them to keep the noise down.

Robert and Paul and Vanessa spread newspapers on their table. They were painting posters about interesting features of New Jersey. Robert's was about the dinosaur fossils that were found there. Paul's was about the Liberty Science Center. Vanessa's was about Great Adventure theme park.

As they set up their paints and brushes, Mrs. Bernthal reminded them that they would have their e-mail buddies' names tomorrow. "Tonight," she said, "start thinking about what you will write in your first note to your e-mail buddy."

Robert had plenty of things to look up even though he had enough information on the dinosaurs in New Jersey to make his report and do his project. Now he wanted to find out more about what it was like in Minnesota, and if there were polar bears in White Bear. He wondered if he would have time to look up everything. He'd better get a chance at the computer tonight. He'd have to let everyone know it was an emergency.

Walking home from school, Robert asked, "What do you suppose kids do in Minnesota?"

"Probably the same things we do here," said Paul.

"You mean like make posters of New Jersey?"

Paul laughed. "No. You know what I mean. There's probably even some kid training his dog to go through an obstacle course."

"No way."

"Way. Why not?"

"Because they have polar bears, not dogs. Did you ever hear of a polar bear doing an obstacle course?"

They laughed for a whole block, cracking themselves up.

"Want to come to my house to do homework?" asked Paul, stopping at his corner.

"Sure," said Robert. He liked doing his homework with Paul. Paul had a computer of his own they could use, and besides, Mrs. Felcher always had something yummy for them after school. Robert felt his stomach rumble just thinking about it.

"Help yourself," said Mrs. Felcher, setting out a plate of Robert's favorite— homemade brownies. She poured milk for them as they talked about their e-mail buddies project.

They each dove for a brownie.

"We have to look up Minnesota first," said Paul, before he stuffed a brownie into his mouth.

"I went to Minnesota once," said Mrs. Felcher. The boys stopped chewing.

"YOU DID?" said Paul.

"Yes, I did. I went ice fishing with a friend. . . ."

"What's ice fishing?"

"When a lake freezes in Minnesota, people go out on the frozen lake, make a hole in the ice, and fish through the hole."

"I thought Eskimos did that," said Paul.

"They probably do," said Mrs. Felcher. "But so do Minnesotans, apparently."

"Mom! We're learning about Minnesota for school," said Paul. "Can you tell us more?"

Mrs. Felcher stopped and sat down at the table, the milk carton still in her hand.

"I can't tell you all about Minnesota, but I can tell you about ice fishing."

112

"Great!" said Robert. That was the part
he wanted to hear, anyway.

"I was in college. It was Christmas
vacation, and my boyfriend . . ."

"Your boyfriend?" Paul's eyes were
bugging out of his head.

"Yes, I had boyfriends before I met
your father," she answered smoothly.

113

"Anyway, my boyfriend, Dan, invited me to visit his family over the holidays, since my own family was traveling. It was my second year in college. Dan took me ice fishing. We drove out on the frozen lake in his dad's RV."

Paul's head spun to face Robert, and Robert's head spun to face Paul. Their mouths hung open.

"How could he drive an RV on the lake?" asked Paul. "Even if it was frozen, the ice could break and the truck might fall in!"

"I think that ice was pretty thick. There were lots of vehicles out on the frozen lake. And I didn't see one fall in!"

They laughed.

Mrs. Felcher continued. "It was bitter cold. We were bundled up in lots of heavy clothing, but it was still cold. Dan drove us out to his house on the lake. . . ."

"Wait. You drove on the frozen lake to his house?" asked Robert.

"Yes, to a little wooden house built on the ice. It had a hole in the floor, and that's where they did their fishing."

"Wow!" said Paul.

"Yeah," said Robert. He took another bite of his brownie as he listened.

"Didn't you freeze, anyway, out in that cold place?" asked Paul.

"Well, believe it or not," said Mrs. Felcher. "Dan built a fire right in the little house on the ice."

"How come it didn't melt the ice?" asked Robert.

"I guess the ice was so thick a little fire couldn't melt it," said Mrs. Felcher. "It kept us from freezing. It was fun, but I never did catch any fish. Dan did, though. We ate them for dinner that night."

"That's so amazing," said Robert.

"Thanks, Mom," said Paul, wiping his mouth with a napkin, then balling it up and leaving it on his plate.

"My pleasure," said Mrs. Felcher. The boys got up to go upstairs. "Don't forget to call your mom to let her know that you're here, Robert," she called after them.

Robert called his mom to tell her he was doing homework at Paul's house. "And Mom?" he said, before he hung up. "I really need the computer tonight to do homework."

"O.K., Robbie. No problem."

That was easier than he thought.

Paul turned on the computer. He checked out Minnesota for the usual major products and population figures, and they both copied them into their notebooks. He checked out Lake Superior and ice fishing. There were pictures of ice houses on the frozen lake.

Finally, he found a Web site for White Bear. "Hey, look," he said. "It says it's a suburb of St. Paul. Let's look up St. Paul." He typed in the words.

"Listen to this!" he shouted. "There's a mall that's a mile square. It's called The Mall of America, and there's a roller coaster inside it!" Robert went over to see. He had seen a carousel for little kids in one of the malls in New Jersey, but this was a regular-size roller coaster.

"That's amazing," he said. "Can I type in a question?"

"Sure." Paul got up and let Robert sit at the computer.

Robert typed in: WERE THERE DINOSAURS IN MINNESOTA?

The first site was one about a couple of paleontologists who had found new dinosaur bones and had dug them up and brought them to the Science Museum of Minnesota. The scientists were from St. Paul.

Minnesota was beginning to look pretty interesting.

White Bear

"**S**usanne Lee, your buddy is Denise," said Mrs. Bernthal. "Andrew, yours is Gordon. And Brian, your buddy is Dave. Please write these names in your notebooks."

Robert didn't know why he felt so excited as the names were called out. Mrs. Bernthal had written on the chalkboard:

Mrs. Gripentrog's class
Willow Lane School
White Bear, Minnesota

Wow. They were going to have buddies who lived all the way over in the middle and at the top of the United States.

Paul's buddy was Jeff. Vanessa's was Meggie. At last, Robert heard his buddy's name called: Kirby. Kirby. Now that his buddy had a name, Robert wanted to know more about him.

Was he a farm kid? Did he like dinosaurs? What was his school like? Was Mrs. Gripentrog anything like Mrs. Bernthal?

Mrs. Bernthal called for their attention. "Class, for tonight's homework, get started on your first letter to your e-mail buddy."

"We have homework already," said Pamela.

"This is in addition to the reports due on Friday. I'll look your letters over before you send them out to be sure the spelling is correct and your manners are in good shape." She winked at them.

"Here are some topics you can include in your e-mails as you introduce yourselves to your buddies." She wrote on the chalkboard as she called them out:

Name (first name only)
Your nickname, if you have one
Family
Pets
School
Teacher
Best friend
Hobbies
Chores that you do
Books you've read
Interesting places in your state
Places you've visited outside your state
Your favorite things
River Edge

"All that?" cried Lester. "I'm glad I didn't sign up."

"You don't have to write everything in one e-mail," Mrs. Bernthal told the class.

"Save some for next time. As for those of you who do not have e-mail buddies . . ." She looked directly at Lester. "I expect you to learn all you can about Minnesota, anyway. Remember your reports are due Friday."

Math and music and reading kept Robert from thinking about his e-mail buddy for the rest of the day. But once they got to Paul's house and were on the computer, they looked up White Bear. That got him thinking again. The pictures showed a lake with the same name and lots of snow and ice sports.

"Hey! Maybe they do snowboarding!" cried Robert.

"Yeah," said Paul, equally excited. "You think Minnesota is like Vermont?" They had both been to Vermont to ski and snow-board with Paul's family.

"Could be," said Robert. He continued to surf.

The next pictures were in summertime. People were swimming in the lake.

"There are no pictures of polar bears," said Paul.

"Maybe they lived there a long time ago," suggested Robert. "Or maybe there are white regular bears," he added.

They surfed a long time until they remembered they had to write their e-mail letters.

"OK. I'll print out what we found so far." Paul clicked a few buttons, and the printer started up. "We can write while the stuff is printing." He got up to give Robert the first turn.

"No, you go first," Robert said. He still hadn't figured out exactly what to say to Kirby. It would help to see Paul do his.

Paul opened his notebook to see Mrs. Bernthal's list of what they could write about. He began typing:

> Dear Jeff,
>   My name is Paul. I am in the third grade. Mrs. Bernthal is my teacher. She is really nice.

Robert read over Paul's shoulder. "Doesn't he know your name already?"

"Oh, yeah," said Paul, deleting the first sentence.

Paul continued.

I have a mom, a dad, and a little
brother, Nick, who is four. I'm eight ,
but I'll be nine in a couple of weeks.
I like to ride my bike with my friend,
Robert. I like to draw, especially
spaceships and rockets.

Robert was glad to see he was mentioned in Paul's e-mail to Jeff.

Paul tried a few more sentences, deleted some and started again, until he had what he wanted. Robert thought his letter sounded really good.

When they checked the clock, it was just about time for Robert to go home.

"Rats!" said Paul. "You should have done yours first. What are you going to do?"

"That's O.K.," said Robert. "I'm just going to tell everyone this is an emergency. I'm going to get the computer tonight or else!"

Paul laughed. "Or else what?" he said.

"Or else I'm in big trouble!" Robert answered. They cracked up again.

On the way home, Robert couldn't help laughing. Even his best friend had turned out to be a computer hog!

From Bad to Worse

R obert's dad seemed especially cheerful at dinner. "So how is everyone?" he asked, rather jovially, as they sat down at the table.

Tonight there was a platter of roast chicken. Robert's mouth watered, it smelled so good. The bags in the kitchen had Big Tex Bar-B-Q printed on them, so he knew his mom didn't make it, but that was O.K. The stuff she made wasn't all that good. Of course, he was too polite to say that to her, but they were all pretty happy when the food was made by someone else.

Robert's mom had cut the chicken into pieces with the kitchen scissors. A bucket of fries, a tub of coleslaw, and a plateful of corn bread was on the table.

But that wasn't why Robert's dad seemed so happy. "I finally heard," he told them, "that I got my sabbatical." He helped himself to a large chunk of chicken.

"What's a sabbatical?" asked Robert, sucking on a fry.

Charlie was making farting noises as he squeezed catsup from the plastic bottle, but he stopped to hear his dad's answer.

"It's time off from work," said Robert's dad. "For six months."

"Like a vacation?"

"Sort of," his dad said. "But I have to do something related to my work, even though I don't have to teach while I'm on it."

Robert's mom added, "Your father is going to write a book."

Really? Robert never knew his dad was a writer.

"A math book," his father added, smiling. "It will be about teaching high school math by combining different types of math, like geometry and trigonometry as a single discipline, or algebra, geometry, and trigonometry in one course."

That sounded like the worst book in the world. Who would read it? But Robert couldn't let his dad know what he thought. He'd probably find out himself.

"That's great, Dad," he said, spearing a drumstick.

"Yeah, Dad," Charlie agreed. "That's awesome." Robert wondered if he was faking it, too.

"Well, I don't know how great or awesome it is, but it's going to be fun."

Fun! Robert would never understand how his dad could think of math as fun, but he knew he really did. Weird.

As everyone added their news to the conversation, Robert said that he had homework to do tonight that involved the computer. Could he please use it for at least an hour? Sure, everyone agreed.

He told them about Kirby and the e-mail buddy program.

"Minnesota," said his dad. "I knew someone from Minnesota once."

"Really?" said Robert.

"Yes, we roomed together at college. He was a very nice fellow."

"Did he tell you about ice fishing?" asked Robert.

"No, I don't think he did," said his dad. "Why?"

"It's what people do in Minnesota. They make little houses out on the frozen lakes and go fishing through a little hole in the floor." Robert felt proud that he could tell his dad about ice fishing.

Everyone thought that was pretty interesting. While his mom put chocolate pudding in front of each of them for dessert, the conversation went on about ice fishing. Finally, Robert had to excuse himself to work on his e-mail to Kirby.

Robert sat at the computer and turned it on. He pulled up a search screen and typed in his favorite word: DINOSAURS. Then he added IN MINNESOTA. Lights flashed across the screen, first green, then the whole screen went black. Robert turned off the computer and turned it on again. The same thing happened, but this time, it happened even before he typed in the word DINOSAURS.

"Mom!" Robert called. "Mom! Something's wrong with the computer!"

Robert's mom came upstairs. She fiddled with it a bit, but ended up calling Robert's dad. He fiddled with the computer, too, and then Charlie tried what he knew. Nothing worked.

"I'm so sorry, Robert," his mom finally said. "The computer died. We'll have to take it in to the computer store."

Back in his room, Robert wondered if he could take a sabbatical from school, like his dad did.

He took his mechanical T-rex down from the windowsill and turned it on. He watched as the dinosaur walked into walls, over a slipper, then got stuck behind the leg of a chair, flashing its fierce eyes, moving its heavy legs in the air, but going nowhere.

That's pretty much how Robert felt. Finally, he picked up his notebook and pencil and wrote until he fell asleep.

The Letter

In class the next morning, the children went up to Mrs. Bernthal's desk to turn in their e-mail letters.

Robert tore his letter to Kirby out of his notebook. It was written in pencil in longhand. He read it over one more time.

Dear Kirby,

I know this should be an e-mail, but our computer is busted. Even when it's O.K. I hardly get to use it because I live with three computer hogs. My mom, my dad, and my brother.

He stopped and looked at that first paragraph again. Then he added "oink, oink" and smiled.

> I am 9 years old and I'm in 3rd grade. My teacher is Mrs. Bernthal.
>
> My favorite subjects are recess and lunch. Ha-ha. Our class has a ribbon snake. Her name is Sally. She is two feet and one inch long. My best friend is Paul. He is four feet six inches long. Ha-ha.
>
> Do you have pets? I have one dog, one tarantula, two turtle doves, and a partridge in a pear tree. Ha-ha. Just kidding. I don't have a partridge in a pear tree.
>
> I may become a dog trainer. I'm teaching my dog to be a wonder dog.
>
> I'm glad Minnesota has ice fishing. It sounds like fun. We don't have ice fishing in New Jersey. We have bowling and a skating rink.
>
> Do you like dinosaurs? New Jersey

had the first dinosaur bones found in
America.

Please write to me. I will check the
computer even if I have to tie up the hogs.
Ha-ha.

Your friend,

Robert

He read it through one more time. This time he added "She is nice" after the sentence about Mrs. Bernthal.

Finally, he went up and handed his letter to her.

Mrs. Bernthal took his letter and stared at it. "You wrote this in longhand?"

Uh-oh. He probably did it all wrong.

"Thank you, Robert," she said.

Mrs. Bernthal asked them to do page 24 in their math workbooks, while she corrected their letters. As they struggled with the problems, she sat at her desk, making little marks on their homework papers with a blue pencil. Robert was not a great speller. A lot of those marks were probably on his paper.

He tried to concentrate on his math. That was never easy. It was especially hard to do problems. If a farmer had two bushels of potatoes that weighed twenty pounds and had to split them three ways, how many pounds would be in each portion? Well, if Kirby did turn out to live on a farm maybe he could just ask him! He laughed to himself.

Mrs. Bernthal took them through their workbook problems and came around to see how they worked them out. She made two corrections on Robert's page.

"Now," she said, going back to her desk. "Let's talk about your letters to your buddies in White Bear."

Robert slid down in his chair.

"This, class, is Robert's letter."

Oh no. She held up his letter.

"I'm going to read it to you."

Robert slid down even further. Mrs. Bernthal read the letter aloud.

The class giggled at some parts. Robert wished he could make himself invisible.

When she finished reading the letter, Mrs. Bernthal sat on the edge of her desk.

"This, class, is a good letter. Notice, please, that it is written in longhand. We haven't even finished learning cursive yet, so you can imagine how long it took Robert to write this."

She looked at Robert. "I assume you wrote this by hand because you did not have access to a computer."

Robert nodded but felt his cheeks get red. He thought of all the erasures he had made and how many times he had to do the page over.

"I think this letter shows amazing resourcefulness." She wrote the word RESOURCEFULNESS on the chalkboard. "You can look that word up tonight," she added.

Robert could hardly sit still all day. When the bell finally rang at three o'clock, he and Paul were out of there in a flash. They started to walk but soon broke into a run. At Paul's corner, Robert dropped his book bag and said, "Wait!"

While Paul watched in amazement, Robert attempted a cartwheel, but landed on his backside. They laughed so hard, Robert could hardly get up again.

Kirby

All week, they worked long and hard, learning about their e-mail buddies in White Bear. Those who didn't have buddies worked on maps and posters about Minnesota. Lester was doing one on ice fishing. The truck on the frozen lake looked very much like his dad's trash removal truck.

Mrs. Gripentrog sent pictures to Robert's class. She didn't look like Mrs. Bernthal. She had short dark hair and was almost always on the floor with the kids in the pictures. But her classroom looked

139

just as interesting as Mrs. Bernthal's. There were always kids on their stomachs on the floor, reading.

One of the White Bear kids, Wendy, wrote that Mrs. Gripentrog played weird music. "But you get used to it after a while, and it's not so bad, really." Another, Audrey, said they had computers in their classroom, which made Robert just a little bit jealous. His classroom had only one; the rest were in the Media Center.

Gordon told them they were not Eskimos and there were no polar bears, but he and his dad went ice fishing every winter in their van. They didn't have an ice house. There were holes cut right in the floor of the van.

Robert was the only one who had not heard from his e-mail buddy. Mrs. Bernthal had liked Robert's longhand letter so much, she had mailed it like a regular letter, with a stamp and everything, so it took longer to get to Kirby than e-mail.

Mrs. Bernthal was really good about seeing that Robert got time at their classroom computer each day. He found lots of information for his report. But best of all, he learned that a couple of people from Minnesota had made one of the most recent dinosaur discoveries. He couldn't wait to see if Kirby knew about them.

At last, a letter arrived for Robert. It was from Kirby, addressed to Robert at Clover Hill Elementary School. He read it slowly.

Dear Robert,

I got your letter and I'm sorry your computer is busted. My mom said it was only fair I write to you in longhand

*because you had to, but I hope your
computer gets fixed soon. E-mail is a lot
faster, and I have chores to do.*

Robert was just imagining Kirby milking the cows when he read further.

*I get up at 5 a.m. to do my paper
route. Then I exercise Loki, my golden
retriever. We run a mile together every
morning, rain or shine—or snow.*

*There's regular stuff, too, like taking
the trash out to the curb and feeding Loki.
I clean the hamster cage every week.*

Do you have chores? What are they?

Curb! Paper route! That was no farm. It sounded just like his neighborhood in River Edge. And Kirby had pets, too! He read on.

Kirby sounded pretty interesting. And it was really nice that he wrote him in longhand. There was just one problem. Kirby never mentioned dinosaurs.

At Last!

Working on the obstacle course after school, Robert stopped and sat down with Huck.

"What's the matter, boy? Don't you want to do your tricks?" He tossed a ball to Huckleberry and had a game of catch. Huck caught the ball a couple of times, then let it sit there while he came over to Robert and plopped himself down on Robert's feet.

"I can't get up and work with you if you sit on my feet," said Robert. "Are you trying to tell me something?"

Charlie came out to the yard. "This is quite a setup," he said. "What are you trying to do, exactly?"

Robert told him about the dog training video. "I'm training Huck to be a wonder dog—you know, one of those dogs who goes through obstacle courses without being afraid."

"Hmmm. How's it working?" asked Charlie.

"It's not," Robert replied.

Charlie went around looking at the equipment. There was a tunnel made out of a plastic trash can with the bottom cut out, the step stool from the kitchen sitting next to a wooden crate. Stretched from the tree to the house was a clothesline. "Well, it's not because you haven't set up a good obstacle course," he said.

Robert rarely got any kind of praise from Charlie, so he was thrilled that his brother was taking such an interest.

"But Huck isn't interested," Robert said. "He'd rather chase squirrels."

"That's too bad," said Charlie, "but some dogs just aren't cut out for athletics. Just like kids."

Robert wondered if Charlie was taking a swipe at him for his notorious lack of sports ability. Charlie was considered a jock. Robert could hardly catch a ball, except when he played with Huckleberry.

Charlie kept walking around the obstacle course. "Nice job," he said. "Maybe you need to do easier tricks with Huck before trying to teach him harder ones."

"Yeah, maybe," Robert said.

Charlie didn't seem to be teasing this time. He was really smart, even though sometimes he could be annoying. Easier tricks. Hmmm. He'd have to tell that to Paul.

When they sat down to dinner, Mom spilled the news before Dad had a chance. "Boys," she said, "we're getting a new computer."

Robert, shocked, could hardly speak. "Seriously?" he finally said.

"All right!" said Charlie. "When?"

"Your father and I and the computer shop technician had a serious talk," said Robert's mom, waving the flyer Robert had given her about a sale on computers. "The old computer is hardly worth repairing, but we'll keep it going as a spare. We really do need a new computer in this family, one that you kids have more access to for your schoolwork."

"Hooray!" said Robert, waving his fork.

"Don't wave sharp objects, Robert," said his mom immediately.

"Sorry," he muttered. He put the fork down. "But that's great news!"

"And I'll need computer time, too," said Robert's dad. "I'll be writing a book, remember, so having a computer to do it with is important."

"And my business still requires the use of a computer to make those travel reservations," his mom added. "Otherwise I have to go in to the office every day."

"So, doesn't that mean we're back to where we started, with everyone hogging the machine?" asked Robert.

"Well, we'll try to take the hog out of it," said Robert's dad. "I made up a plan."

Groan. Robert's dad loved to make plans and maps and charts.

"I'll post it on the refrigerator," he continued. "Each of us will have hours at the computer that nobody else can have."

That sounded good, so far.

"And if anyone has an emergency, we'll have a meeting and donate our time as much as we can to the person in crisis."

It sounded too good to be true. But if it worked . . .

Robert's dad explained that he would be home full-time starting in the fall. He was going to write during the day, when the boys were in school. His mom said she would probably be O.K. on the spare computer, so it was just working out the hours after school and in the evening for Robert and Charlie.

Robert started thinking about the next e-mail he would write. He'd start with: *Dear Kirby, I have a T-rex in my room. Do you like dinosaurs?*

Later, after Robert's favorite TV program, the *Instant Millionaire* show, was over, he went upstairs to call Paul.

"Guess what?" he asked. Paul couldn't guess, so Robert went on, "We're getting a new computer."

"That's great," Paul said. "How come?"

Robert explained. "And guess what else?" he asked.

"What?" said Paul

"Charlie came out to look at the obstacle course, and he gave me a good suggestion."

"For real?"

"Yes, for real. I was surprised, too. He said to work with easier tricks first, then do harder ones."

"That sounds right," said Paul.

"Yeah," Robert agreed. He suddenly felt relaxed. "You know something? It isn't Huck who has to learn about the obstacle course. It's us."

Paul laughed. "I think you're right," he said. "Do you want to jump through the hoop or shall I?"

"Thanks. I'll take the lawn chairs," said Robert. Once again, they cracked themselves up.

BARBARA SEULING is a well-known author of fiction and nonfiction books for children, including several books about Robert. She divides her time between New York City and Vermont.

PAUL BREWER likes to draw gross, silly situations, which is why he enjoys working on books about Robert so much. He lives in San Diego, California, with his wife and two daughters. He is the author and illustrator of *You Must Be Joking! Lots of Cool Jokes, Plus 17 1/2 Tips for Remembering, Telling, and Making Up Your Own Jokes.*